What's In Your Heaven?

Paige Priscilla
Illustrated by Victor Guiza

Outskirts Press, Inc.
http://www.outskirtspress.com

Paperback ISBN: 978-1-9772-2564-1
Hardback ISBN: 978-1-9772-2565-8

Library of Congress Control Number: 2020905119

Illustrations by: Victor Guiza.
Illustrations © 2020 Outskirts Press, Inc. All rights reserved - used with permission.

Outskirts Press and the "OP" logo are trademarks belonging to Outskirts Press, Inc.

PRINTED IN THE UNITED STATES OF AMERICA

This Book Belongs to:

After a blessed life here on the ground,

way up high eternity is found

when it is meant to be,

a beautiful light you shall see

Beyond this light are the Pearly Gates,

whatever you desire is what waits

Heaven will be all your favorite things—

because your such an angel, you even get wings

If style is your passion,

your Heaven will have all the latest fashion

If you love to paint day and night,

a Heaven of acrylics would suit you just right

If gaming is your gig,

you shall have a video screen

THIS BIG

If cats are what make your world complete,

you can bet God gave them a special suite

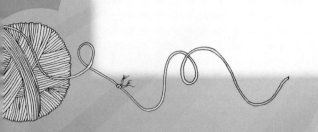

All you must do is use your imagination—

It will be like a permanent vacation

With man's best friend,

that is the eternity I will spend

First, I will thank my savior

for all He has given me

Then this is what I will see...

A lazy dog curled up on a cloud

A frisky dog running and barking excited and loud

A hunting dog chasing birds

and squirrels to his heart's content

And a bashful teacup pup,

but I don't know where she went

Napping under the willow tree is a hound—

because of him, many who were lost are found

Sitting proudly upon the fire truck

is a Dalmatian they named Lady Luck

No matter how sad or ill one may have been,

in Heaven all are happy and healthy again

In a Heaven of mostly canine,

when the time comes, it will also be mine

So, if there are people or pets that you miss,

look to the sky, and blow them a kiss

Lightning Source UK Ltd.
Milton Keynes UK
UKRC011548060820
367800UK00001B/5